9355

NORTH COUNTY JOINT UNION SCHOOL
500 SPRING GROVE RD.
HOLLISTER, CA 95023

A NOTE TO PARENTS

Reading Aloud with Your Child

Research shows that reading books aloud is the single most valuable support parents can provide in helping children learn to read.

- Be a ham! The more enthusiasm you display, the more your child will enjoy the book.
- Run your finger underneath the words as you read to signal that the print carries the story.
- Leave time for examining the illustrations more closely; encourage your child to find things in the pictures.
- Invite your youngster to join in whenever there's a repeated phrase in the text.
- Link up events in the book with similar events in your child's life.
- If your child asks a question, stop and answer it. The book can be a means to learning more about your child's thoughts.

Listening to Your Child Read Aloud

The support of your attention and praise is absolutely crucial to your child's continuing efforts to learn to read.

- If your child is learning to read and asks for a word, give it immediately so that the meaning of the story is not interrupted. DO NOT ask your child to sound out the word.
- On the other hand, if your child initiates the act of sounding out, don't intervene.
- If your child is reading along and makes what is called a miscue, listen for the sense of the miscue. If the word "road" is substituted for the word "street," for instance, no meaning is lost. Don't stop the reading for a correction.
- If the miscue makes no sense (for example, "horse" for "house"), ask your child to reread the sentence because you're not sure you understand what's just been read.
- Above all else, enjoy your child's growing command of print and make sure you give lots of praise. *You are your child's first teacher—and the most important one. Praise from you is critical for further risk-taking and learning.*

—Priscilla Lynch
Ph.D., New York University
Educational Consultant

Library of Congress Cataloging-in-Publication Data

Gave, Marc.
    Monkey see, monkey do / by Marc Gave; illustrated by Jacqueline Rogers.
      p.   cm. — (Hello reader)
    Summary: Rhyming text relates the antics of monkeys that play all day.
    ISBN 0-590-45801-9
    [1. Monkeys — Fiction. 2. Play — Fiction. 3. Stories in rhyme.]
    I. Rogers, Jacqueline, ill. II. Title. III. Series.
PZ8.3.G22Mo   1993
[E] — dc20   91-45443
                                            CIP
_T/535_ •   AC

2019181716   6 7/9

Printed in the U.S.A.   **24**

First Scholastic printing, January 1993

Monkey See, Monkey Do

by Marc Gave
Illustrated by Jacqueline Rogers

Hello Reader! — Level 1

SCHOLASTIC INC.

New York   Toronto   London   Auckland   Sydney

Monkey me.
Monkey you.

Monkey see.
Monkey do.

Monkey on the left.

Monkey on the right.

Monkey in the middle.

Monkey out of sight.

Monkey up a tree.
Monkey on the ground.

Monkeys in a bunch,
monkeying around.

Monkeys stay.

Monkeys go.

Monkeys go fast.

Monkeys go slow.

Monkeys walk.

Monkeys run.

Monkeys have some monkey fun.

Monkeys bend.

Monkeys reach.

Monkeys lie
along the beach.

Monkeys swim.
Monkeys row.

Monkeys swing
to and fro.

Monkeys play
while the sky is light.

Monkeys sleep through the night.

Good night.